Enid Blyton

Merry
Mister Meddle

Text illustrations by Diana Catchpole
Cover illustration by Maggie Downer

D1323785

AWARD PUBLICATIONS LIMITED

Enid Blyton's Happy Days!

Snowball the Pony

Bimbo and Topsy

Run-About's Holiday

The Adventures of Binkle and Flip

Binkle and Flip Misbehave

Mister Meddle's Mischief

Mister Meddle's Muddles

Merry Mister Meddle

You're a Nuisance Mister Meddle

Collect all the titles in the series!

The Adventures of
Mr Pink-Whistle

Mr Pink-Whistle
Has Some Fun

Mr Pink-Whistle's
Party

Mr Pink-Whistle
Interferes

Hello
Mr Twiddle!

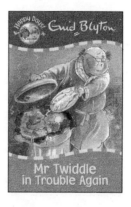

Mr Twiddle
in Trouble Again

Don't Be Silly,
Mr Twiddle!

Mr Twiddle
in Trouble Again

Shuffle
the Shoemaker

For further information on Enid Blyton please visit *www.blyton.com*

ISBN 978-1-84135-662-4

Illustrations copyright © Award Publications Limited

First published 1954 by George Newnes

First published by Award Publications Limited 2004
This edition first published 2010

Published by Award Publications Limited,
The Old Riding School, The Welbeck Estate,
Worksop, Nottinghamshire, S80 3LR

11 2

Printed in the United Kingdom

Contents

Chapter 1

Meddle and the Mice

'These tiresome mice!' said Meddle's Aunt Jemima, looking into the larder. 'They've been all over the place, look! Nibbling this, that and the other.'

'What about getting a cat, Aunt?' asked Meddle. 'Wouldn't that be a good idea? She'd soon get rid of the mice for you.'

'You know I don't like cats,' said his aunt. 'Now, Meddle, I'm going out to tea, so please behave yourself till I come back again. I'll be back about eight, and we'll have supper then.'

Off she went. Meddle heaved a sigh of relief when she had gone. Aunt Jemima was always finding fault with him. It was nice to be able to sit down and put his feet up on the mantelpiece and read a book and eat as many peppermints as he liked.

As he sat there reading, he heard a scrabbling sound from the larder. Those mice again!

Meddle put down his book and thought.

'What about a mouse trap?' he said. 'I know where there is one – out in the shed. I'll get it and set it with a bit of bacon and a bit of cheese. I'll catch those mice for Aunt Jemima. Won't she be pleased?'

He went to fetch the trap. As he came out of the shed with it, the large black cat from next door came up to him and rubbed against his legs.

'Puss, Puss,' said Meddle and bent to stroke the cat. Then a bright idea came to him.

'Puss, would you like to sit in our larder and catch a few mice?' he asked. The cat purred. She went indoors with Meddle, and sat down by the fire to wash herself.

'I'll just set this trap, Puss,' said Meddle, 'and then you can go into the larder with it. What with you and the trap, the mice will have a very bad time!'

He went to the larder. He took the cheese from the dish and broke a bit off. He put it in

the trap. Then he unwrapped the bacon and cut a bit of fat from it. He put that on the hook too, and then carefully set the trap. He put it down on the floor.

'There!' he said. 'If that doesn't catch a mouse I'll be surprised!'

He forgot to put the lid back on the cheese-dish. He forgot to wrap the bacon up again. Meddle could never think of little things like that!

He called to the cat. 'Here, Puss! Come and watch for mice here. Come along.'

The cat didn't come. So Meddle went and fetched her and put her firmly down in the larder. Then he shut the door.

It was cold in the larder. The cat didn't like it. She didn't care about mice either, for she was well-fed and never bothered herself to catch them. She mewed and scratched at the door.

'You catch a few mice, and I'll let you out!' said Meddle, and put his feet up on the

mantelpiece again. The cat seemed to settle down and there was no sound of either mouse or cat from the larder.

Meddle made himself some tea after a bit and got the biscuit tin. He wasn't going to bother to cut himself bread and butter! He finished all the biscuits in the tin. Then he washed up his tea things, and went back to read again. But he fell fast asleep, and only woke up when he heard his Aunt Jemima coming in.

'Oh, dear, dear!' she said. 'I missed the bus, and it's half past eight and I'm so hungry. Why, Meddle, you haven't even set the supper! Lay the cloth, quickly.'

She stood before the mirror to take off her hat. Suddenly there came a loud noise from the larder.

'CRASH!'

'Whatever's that?' cried Aunt Jemima.

'Oh – I set a mouse trap there for you,' said Meddle. 'I expect that's the trap catching a mouse!'

'What – a crash like that!' cried his aunt. 'Oh, my goodness – there's another crash – and look, there's milk flowing out under the door! Mice indeed!'

11

She ran to the larder door and opened it. Out shot the big black cat; it jumped out of the window and disappeared. Aunt Jemima stared in horror at the larder.

'How did that cat get in here? Oh, my goodness, it's eaten the meat pie I left for supper – and the fish for breakfast – and it's gobbled up the custard I put ready – and it's upset the milk – and look at all this chewed bacon and nibbled cheese.' How *did* that cat get in here?'

Then she gave a scream. The mouse trap had gone off and nipped her toe. 'What's that? Oh, the mouse trap, Meddle, did you put that cheese and bacon in it?'

'Yes, Aunt,' said Meddle in a small voice.

'Well, why didn't you cover up the cheese-dish and wrap up the bacon?' asked his aunt. 'Didn't you know that even if the cat wasn't there to nibble them, the mice would climb up to the shelves and eat them? They wouldn't bother about the trap, if they could see cheese and bacon up here in plenty!'

'No, Aunt,' said Meddle, edging towards the kitchen door.

'Meddle, how did that cat get in here? Did *you* put it in?' said Aunt Jemima, suddenly.

'The larder window's closed. It couldn't possibly have got in by itself.'

'Well, Aunt Jemima – you see, Aunt – it's like this – after all, a cat does catch mice,' began Meddle. 'And I thought –'

'You thought it would be a very good idea to put that cat into my larder for hours, till it began to get really hungry and eat all our supper!' cried his aunt. 'Come here, Meddle, come here!'

But Meddle was gone! 'Good thing too!' said his aunt. 'There's only supper enough for one – an egg and bread and butter. Just wait till you come in, Meddle, just wait!'

Poor Meddle. He does his best, but it's such a bad best, isn't it?

Chapter 2

Meddle Does the Washing

Meddle was staying with his Aunt Jemima. He didn't like Mondays because it was his aunt's washing day then, and she groaned and grumbled all day long.

'Oh, how dirty you make your shirts, Meddle! Anyone would think you lived in a chimney, they're so black! And look at these hankies of yours! Have you used them to wipe up spilt ink or something?'

'Oh, dear – it's washing day again!' Meddle would think. 'I must really get out of Aunt's way. She grumbles all day long – goodness knows why! There doesn't seem to be anything much in washing. You just get hot water, make a fine lather of soap and get on with it. I'm sure I could do it easily enough without any grumbling!'

He watched his aunt making the lather in the wash-tub. He liked all the bubbly, frothy lather. He dipped his fingers into it. It felt soft and silky.

'The better lather you have, the easier it is to wash the clothes,' said his aunt. 'But it's difficult to get a good, frothy lather these days. Get out of the way, Meddle. You'll have the tub over in a minute.'

Now the next Monday Meddle's aunt had a pain in her back. She sat in her armchair and groaned: 'Oh, dear, oh, dear! I can't do the washing today. I've such a pain in my back. I must do it tomorrow.'

Meddle looked at his aunt in alarm. 'Tomorrow! Oh, no, Aunt. You promised to take me to the fair.'

'Well, washing is more important than going to the fair,' said his aunt.

Meddle didn't think it was at all. He went into the scullery and looked at the pile of washing there. Horrible washing! Now he wouldn't be able to go to the fair!

Then an idea came into his mind. Why shouldn't *he* do the washing? It always looked very easy. And if he got a really fine lather it would be easier still.

'I'll go to Dame Know-all and ask her for a little growing-spell,' thought Meddle. 'I'll pop it into the wash-tub with the lather, and it will grow marvellously so that I can do all the washing in no time at all.'

He went off to Dame Know-all. She was out. Meddle looked round her little shop. Ah – there on a shelf was a bottle marked 'Growing-spells'. Just what he wanted!

He put fifty pence down on the counter, took down the bottle, unscrewed the lid and emptied a small growing-spell into his hand. It was like a tiny blue pea.

He put back the bottle and went out of the shop. He ran back to his aunt's in glee. Aha! It took a clever fellow like him to think how to make washing easy! What a fine soapy lather he could get. How all the dirt would roll out of the clothes when he popped them into the lather and squeezed them!

He peeped in at his aunt. She was still in her chair. She had fallen asleep. Meddle softly closed the door and went into the scullery.

He filled the wash-tub with boiling hot

water and popped in the soap flakes his aunt used. He swished them about with his hand, and a bubbly lather began to rise up in the tub.

Then Meddle put in the little blue growing-spell. It dissolved in the water and made it bluer than before. A little blue steam came up and mixed with the soapy lather.

And the lather began to grow!

Hundreds and hundreds of soapy bubbles began to form in the tub, and frothed out over the side, shining with all the colours of the rainbow.

'Good!' said Meddle, pleased, and he

stuffed all the dirty clothes into the frothing lather. He pushed them down into the hot water, and began to squeeze them. But he couldn't do that for long, because the lather had grown so much that it frothed right up to his face. Bubbles burst and his eyes began to smart. He blew the lather away from his cheeks.

But it went on growing! He had taken a far too powerful growing-spell from the bottle, and thousands and thousands of soapy bubbles were frothing up.

The lather fell out of the tub and went on growing. Soon Meddle was waist-deep in bubbles! He kicked at them.

'Stop growing! That's enough! How can I possibly do the washing when I can't get near the tub? Stop, I tell you!'

But the lather didn't stop. It crept along the floor frothing out beautifully. It grew higher. It sent bubbles all over the top of the table, and on to the gas stove. Gracious, what a sight!

Meddle began to feel alarmed. 'STOP!' he shouted. 'Are you deaf? STOP!'

But the bubbles went on growing by the hundred and frothed about everywhere.

Some of them rolled out of the window. The bubbly lather-stream went through the door into the kitchen. It frothed over the floor there, looking very peculiar indeed. Meddle began to get really frightened. He made his way out of the scullery, where the bubbles were now up to his neck, and found a broom. He attacked the lather with all his might, trying to sweep it back into the scullery, so that he could close the door on it.

But the more he swept, the quicker it grew! It was dreadful. Thank goodness the door into the sitting room was shut. Whatever would his aunt think if she saw a mass of froth creeping into the sitting room?

The larder door was open, and the lather went there, frothing all over the shelves. Oh, dear! It soon hid the meat pie and the cold pudding that Aunt Jemima had planned for dinner that day.

Aunt Jemima slept peacefully in the parlour. She had had a bad night and was glad to rest a little, with a cushion at her back. But when the noise of Meddle sweeping hard in the kitchen came to her ears, she awoke and sat up.

'What's that? What can Meddle be doing?

The kitchen doesn't want sweeping!' she said to herself. She looked at the shut door and wondered if she should call out to Meddle to stop.

And then she saw something very peculiar indeed. A little line of lather was creeping under the door! A little drip of lather was coming through the key-hole! Aunt Jemima started as if she couldn't believe her eyes. What was this strange thing creeping under the door? And whatever was coming through the key-hole? She wondered if she was still asleep and dreaming.

'Meddle,' she called, 'what are you doing?

Open the door. There's something peculiar happening.'

Meddle heard what his aunt said – but he certainly wasn't going to open the door and let all the bubbles into the sitting room! It was quite bad enough already in the kitchen. The froth was almost up to his shoulders. He couldn't even *see* his legs! Sometimes the bubbles went up his nose and made him sneeze and choke. His eyes smarted. He felt very upset.

Aunt Jemima watched the line of bubbles creeping under the door in alarm. As soon as the lather was properly in the sitting room it began to grow very quickly. It frothed up into the air, and Aunt Jemima got out of her chair in fright. What was all this?

She trod through the bubbles and opened the door into the kitchen. That was a terrible mistake! At once a great cloud of soapy bubbles swept over her, and she was almost smothered in them. She screamed.

'Meddle, what *is* this? What's happening? Good gracious, I can hardly see the top of your head!'

'Oh, Aunt, oh, Aunt, it's all because of a growing-spell I put into the wash-tub to make a fine lather,' wept Meddle. 'It won't stop growing now. Oh, what are we to do?'

'Well! Of all the donkeys, you're the biggest, Meddle!' shouted his aunt, trying to make her way through the bubbles. 'Open the garden door! Sweep the lather into the garden. Don't let it fill the house!'

Meddle groped his way to the door, coughing and sneezing. He opened it. A great wave of froth immediately rolled out. More and more followed. It went down the garden path, and all the passers-by stood still in astonishment to see such a sight.

They had to get out of the way of the lather when it got to the hedge. It frothed over it and made its way down the road. Aunt Jemima watched it.

'Won't it ever stop?' said Meddle, really scared.

'It will stop when the growing-spell is worn out,' said his aunt, in a very grim voice.

The spell didn't wear itself out for four hours. By that time the lather had reached the village, and all the children were paddling about in the bubbles, having a lovely time. How they laughed and shouted!

But at last the froth grew smaller and

smaller. The bubbles burst and disappeared and grew no more. By one o'clock there was not a single bubble left. The wonderful lather had gone.

Meddle was terribly hungry by this time. So was his aunt. She went to the larder and looked at the soapy meat pie and the cold pudding. Then she went out to the hen-house and found two newly laid eggs. She brought them back and put them in a saucepan on the stove to boil.

'You can have the pie and the pudding,'

she said to Meddle. But when he tried to eat them, he made a terrible face.

'Oooh! they taste of soap! Can I have an egg, Aunt?'

'There are only two, and I'm having them both,' said his aunt. 'Eat up the pie and the pudding.'

So poor Meddle had to, and they tasted far worse than any medicine he had ever had in his life.

'I shall have to do the washing tomorrow, just as I planned,' said his aunt. 'Next time you want to meddle in anything, Meddle, tell me before you start. It would save such a lot of trouble! As for the fair, don't dare to mention it! It might make me put you into the wash-tub with the dirty washing!'

Chapter 3

Meddle's Treacle Pudding

One day Meddle went to take his aunt some daffodils out of his garden. She wasn't feeling very pleased with him, and he thought it would be a good idea to make her a little present of flowers.

She was delighted. 'Well, there now, Meddle, if that isn't kind of you!' she said. 'You're a silly, meddlesome fellow most of the time, but not always. Stay and have dinner with me.'

'What are you having for dinner?' asked Meddle.

'Cold meat, baked potatoes, and a nice jam sponge pudding,' said his aunt.

'Couldn't you make it a treacle pudding instead?' begged Meddle. 'I do so like treacle puddings.'

'I would, if I'd got any treacle,' said Aunt Jemima. 'But I haven't. Not a drop! So you'll have to make do with a jam sponge pudding if you are going to stay and have dinner with me, Meddle.'

'All right,' said Meddle, and he picked up the morning paper to read whilst his aunt bustled round to do her work. But she didn't like that.

'Now, Meddle, don't you laze about,' she said. 'If you're going to spend the morning with me, you'll have to do something. I can't bear people who laze about.'

'Oh, dear,' said Meddle. 'Well, what do you want me to do?'

'I've got the workmen doing odd jobs in my scullery today,' said Aunt Jemima. 'You go and see if you can help them. Hammer in some nails, or something.'

Meddle wandered off into the scullery, but after he had hammered somebody's fingers, and upset all the tools into the wet sink, the workmen didn't want him any more. Nobody ever wanted Meddle for long!

One of them gave him a little pot with something yellow-brown at the bottom of it.

'Go and put this on the kitchen hob and stir it every now and again,' he said. 'That will keep you out of mischief.'

Meddle took the little pot. He put it on the hot kitchen hob. Then he looked round for something to stir with. He found an old spoon.

By the time he got back to the hob the yellow-brown stuff in the little pot was bubbling nicely. Meddle peered at it.

'My goodness me, if it isn't treacle!' he said. 'Look at that now! A pot full of melting treacle, and Aunt Jemima hasn't any at all.'

He stirred it. It wasn't treacle, of course, it

was glue. But that didn't enter Meddle's head at all. He was sure it was good rich treacle. He stirred it well.

'This would taste lovely on our pudding,' he thought. 'It's just what we want. I wonder if the workmen would mind if I had two big spoonfuls for our pudding. I'll ask them.'

So he popped his head into the scullery and called to them. 'I say, can I have some of this stuff on my pudding, men?'

The workmen thought he was trying to be funny. They laughed. 'Take what you like for your pudding!' called one. 'It's not what *we'd* choose – but if you like it, take it!'

Meddle was delighted. He went to tell his Aunt, but she had gone out shopping. She had left the pudding steaming on the stove. Meddle began to feel hungry. How lovely to have a nice sponge pudding with treacle all over it. Oooooh!

He laid the table. He got the dish ready for the pudding. He took the baked potatoes out of the oven, and wrapped them up in a napkin and put them into a dish to keep hot.

Aunt Jemima was pleased to see all he had done when she got home. She beamed at Meddle. 'Well, well – you *can* be useful when

you try. I'm pleased with you, Meddle. You
shall have two helpings of the pudding.'

Meddle didn't say anything about the
treacle. He thought he would give his aunt a
nice surprise. He left it simmering on the
hob.

Soon Meddle and his aunt were sitting
down to have their dinner. They ate their
cold meat, potatoes and pickles, and then
Aunt Jemima went to get the pudding. Soon
it was on its hot dish, and Aunt Jemima
carried it to the table. 'Now bless us all, if I

haven't forgotten to warm up the jam for the pudding!' she said.

'It's all right,' said Meddle. 'I've got some hot treacle for it! Sit down, Aunt, and I'll get it. It will be *such* a treat!'

He went to get it. He poured some of it out of the glue-pot into a sauceboat, and took it to the table. 'All thick and hot!' he said, and his mouth watered as he thought of the treat in store. He poured half of it over his aunt's pudding. He poured the rest over his own helping.

'It looks a bit peculiar,' said Aunt Jemima, doubtfully. 'And it smells funny, too.'

'It'll *taste* all right!' said Meddle. 'Try it, Aunt Jemima.'

They both took a big spoonful of their pudding, and then made two dreadful faces. Their teeth stuck together. They couldn't chew, they couldn't speak, they couldn't swallow!

Aunt Jemima stumbled to the bathroom to get some water. Meddle's eyes nearly fell out of his head with horror. 'It's glue!' he thought. 'It's glue! Oh, why did I meddle with it? Horrible, horrible, horrible!'

He couldn't say a word, and neither could

his aunt, even after she had drunk glass after glass of water. But she *did* a lot. She chased him round the room sixteen times. Then she chased him out of the house and up the road. Meddle raced away, large tears running down his sticky cheeks.

'Now, then, what's the matter?' said Mr Plod the policeman, meeting Meddle suddenly round a corner. 'What are you in such a hurry for? Just you stop and explain.'

But all that poor Meddle could say was 'Ooof-ooof-ooof!' so he had to go with Mr Plod, who thought he was being rude. And I'm very much afraid he'll have to stay at the police station till the glue is worn off!

Chapter 4

Mister Meddle's New Suit

'Oh, dear – I really do need a new suit!' said Mister Meddle one summer morning, as he looked at himself in the glass. 'My trousers are torn, my coat is dirty, and really I am surprised that my shirt holds together. As for my socks, they are nothing but holes!'

He went to look in his purse. There was five pence there, and that was all.

'Can't buy even a pair of socks with that,' said Mister Meddle. 'I've got to go to tea with Aunt Jemima this afternoon, too. Well, she'll just have to put up with my old clothes!'

He set off to go to tea with his aunt at about three o'clock. He had washed his hands and brushed his hair but he hadn't mended his trousers or darned the holes in his socks. That was much too much trouble.

It was a very windy day indeed. Mister Meddle wished he had a kite to fly. The boys and girls had all got out their kites and were having fun with them. The big windmill on the common was whizzing round and round. Mister Meddle's hat blew off three times, and he got cross.

He picked it up out of the dust and looked at it. 'Now you've got dirty, too!' he said. He brushed it hard with his hand and slapped it against himself. 'I do wish I had some nice clothes. I'm tired of looking like a tramp!'

He climbed over a stile to go across a field. He saw something peculiar flapping along the ground towards him and stared in astonishment.

'What is it? Good gracious! It's a shirt. A blue silk shirt! Now, whatever is it doing dancing about in this field all alone?'

He picked it up. It was exactly his size. 'This is a very strange thing,' said Meddle, and looked all round to see if by chance anyone had dropped the shirt. But there was no one about at all.

Then he saw something else coming

towards him. How strange! This time it was a pair of trousers! They were a bright red, and had stripes of blue running down the sides. Very, very unusual, thought Mister Meddle.

He picked up the trousers and tried them against himself. They seemed just his size. He felt very excited indeed.

'I do believe – yes, I do believe that my wish has come true!' he said to himself. 'I was saying how I wished I had some new clothes – and now here are some dancing across the field to me!'

Then he saw something else – something brightly red, like the trousers, with little blue buttons on the front. A coat! A really beautiful coat! Meddle could hardly believe his eyes.

'What a bit of luck! Here's a coat too. Yes, there's no doubt my wish has come true. And my goodness me, here come a pair of blue socks! I'll look about for some shoes, too – and a new hat would be nice.'

But he couldn't find either shoes or hat. Still, never mind – he had a wonderful set of new clothes, and he meant to put them on at once. So he went into a tumbledown cowshed nearby, took off his old clothes, and put on

the new ones – the fine blue shirt, the red
coat and trousers, and the blue socks. Lovely!

'I wish I could see myself,' thought Meddle.
'I must look awfully grand. What shall I do
with my horrible old clothes? Here, goat, you
can have them!'

A billy-goat had just put his head in at the
shed door. Meddle threw him the clothes.
The goat looked surprised. It sniffed at them,
and then began to chew them up. It didn't

mind what it ate. Meddle's old clothes would make a very good meal indeed!

Meddle went joyfully out of the shed, dressed in blue and red. Whatever would Aunt Jemima say? She would hardly know him!

His aunt stared in surprise when she opened the door to him. 'Meddle! You've been spending far too much money on new clothes! You bad boy.'

'I haven't spent a penny,' said Meddle. 'Aunt, I wished for some new clothes, and they all came dancing up to me!'

'I don't believe a word of it!' said his aunt at once. Meddle looked very hurt.

'I'm telling the truth,' he said. 'They came dancing over the field right to my feet. Don't you think I look nice, Aunt? You're always saying I ought to have new clothes.'

'You look smarter than I've ever seen you,' said Aunt Jemima. 'Come along in to tea. There are some new ginger buns, and some lovely honey from my neighbour's bees. I hope you won't spill it down your new suit!'

Now, in the middle of tea, when Meddle was spreading new honey on his bread, there came a knock at the door. Aunt Jemima went

to open it. Meddle heard someone talking to his aunt in a very worried voice. It was Mrs Buzz, the bee-woman from next door.

'Whatever's the matter with her?' said Meddle to himself. 'Well, all I hope is that she keeps Aunt talking for a long time, then I can have lots of honey.'

He listened again – and then his hair stood up on his head in horror.

'My dear, I pegged them all out on my line, and when I went to take them in, they'd gone!' said Mrs Buzz's voice. 'Quite gone –

the blue shirt, the red trousers and coat, and even the blue socks. What Mr Buzz will say I really *don't* know. I suppose the strong wind blew them away.'

Meddle dropped a blob of honey on his coat; he got such a shock to hear all this that his hand trembled like a jelly. Oh, dear, oh, dear – so that's where his new clothes had come from – Mrs Buzz's clothes-line! Why hadn't he thought of that?

His Aunt Jemima came into the room, looking very stern indeed. Mrs Buzz was

behind her. She gave a scream when she saw Meddle.

'Oh! He's got all the lost clothes on! Oh, the rascal!'

'Meddle! How dare you take clothes off somebody's clothes-line?' said his aunt, in such a terrible voice that Meddle shook and shivered.

'I didn't. They danced over the field to me,' said poor Meddle, in a shaky voice.

'Take them off. Put on your old clothes and give these back to Mrs Buzz,' commanded his aunt.

'I c-c-can't,' said Meddle. 'I gave my old clothes to the billy-g-g-goat to eat!'

'You're a wicked fellow!' said Mrs Buzz. 'I'm off to get the policeman!'

She ran out of the room, and poor Meddle was terribly frightened. He jumped out of the window, and began to run home as fast as he could.

Just as he was getting over the stile, he saw a man coming towards him. As soon as he saw him, this man gave a loud shout, and rushed at the surprised Mister Meddle. He gave him such a blow that Meddle fell back over the stile again.

'You've got my clothes on!' shouted the man. It was Mr Buzz! 'How dare you! You give them to me at once!'

Meddle got up and raced away. Mr Buzz looked so fierce that he was afraid of him. Meddle rushed to the cowshed and disappeared inside. The goat was still there, chewing what looked like a heap of rags.

'Shoo, goat, shoo!' cried Meddle. The goat looked surprised, and backed away with a bit of Meddle's shirt hanging from its mouth. Meddle groaned.

'Is that all that's left of my shirt? And, oh dear, look at this coat – both sleeves have been eaten – and there's no sign of my socks – and you've eaten one leg of my trousers right up to the knee.'

The goat then heard Mr Buzz coming and moved to the door. It felt cross. Was someone else coming to disturb it at its meal? When Mr Buzz peered round the door the goat ran at him and butted him hard. He rolled over and over on the grass outside.

Meddle hurriedly took off his new clothes and put on his poor sleeveless coat and his half-eaten trousers. He couldn't put on a shirt or socks because they had been eaten.

Then he went cautiously to the door.

The goat was having a fine game with poor Mr Buzz! It was dancing all round him, butting him whenever he tried to get up. Mr Buzz was getting angrier and angrier.

Meddle shouted to Mr Buzz: 'Look, here are your clothes! You can get them when the goat lets you!' He threw down the clothes and then raced off home, looking more like a tramp than ever, in his half-chewed, ragged coat and trousers.

He looked at himself in the glass when he got home. 'I can't go out like this! I'll have to

put on an overall and go to work somewhere, to earn money for new things. Just as I'm feeling lazy, too!'

He wondered if Mr and Mrs Buzz would come along with the policeman, and whether his aunt would come to scold him. Meddle thought it very likely indeed.

He found his overall, put it on, packed a little bag, and then went to catch a bus to the next town. He locked his door and put the key in his pocket.

'I'll get a job miles away!' he said, 'even if it means working hard and wearing an overall for weeks till I can buy a new suit.'

So, when Aunt Jemima came along to scold him she couldn't find him, and when Mr and Mrs Buzz came with a policeman he wasn't there.

Poor Meddle! He won't believe in wishes coming true again, will he?

Chapter 5

Meddle's Good Turns

Aunt Jemima was very cross with Meddle. He had been staying with her for a few days, and had managed to upset everybody, even the cat.

He had made the cook cross because he had gone into her larder at night and eaten all the jam tarts she had made for the next day's dinner. He had upset the gardener by borrowing his best spade and leaving it somewhere where it couldn't be found.

And he had upset the cat by treading three times on its tail in one day.

'You are very unkind, Meddle,' said his aunt.

'I'm *not*,' said Meddle. 'It's the cat that's untidy – leaving her tail about all over the place for people to tread on. I believe she does it on purpose.'

Then he upset his aunt by telling her not to bother about watering her plants, he'd do it for her – and he took the wrong jug, and used up all the day's milk to water the plants.

'But couldn't you *see* it was milk when it came pouring out?' said his aunt, exasperated.

'I didn't look,' said Meddle. 'And if I *had* looked and seen it, I should just have thought your water was a funny colour, that's all. I took the jug you told me.'

'No, you didn't,' said his aunt in her very crossest voice. 'Meddle, I feel I'm going to shout at you very soon. Very, very soon. I can feel myself getting angrier and angrier. I can –'

Meddle backed away in alarm. 'I'm sorry, Aunt Jemima. Really, I am. I'm going out now so I shan't worry you any more this morning.'

'Well, Meddle, you'd better turn over a new leaf and try to help people instead of hindering them,' said his aunt. 'You go out, and when you come back you just tell me all the *good* things you've done. If you've any to tell I might not feel so angry towards you.'

Meddle put on his hat and went out in a
hurry, treading on the cat's tail once more.
The cat spat and dug its claws into his leg.
Meddle howled, leapt into the air, and fell
down the steps.

His aunt slammed the door and comforted
the cat. The cook put her head into the hall.

'Has he gone?' she said. 'Ha, that's a pity.
I've just discovered that a meat-pie is missing,
and I've got a rolling-pin here to punish the
thief.'

'He's gone,' said Aunt Jemima. 'He's going to turn over a new leaf, and do some good deeds for a change.'

'I'll believe that when I hear he's done some,' said the cook, and disappeared with the cat close behind her.

Meddle wandered down the street, a big hole in his sock where the cat had scratched him. He looked very solemn. He really and truly would do a good deed – if he could find one to do. There were always so many to do when he didn't want to – but now that he wanted to, it was difficult to find one.

He saw an old lady crossing the road with a basket full of goods. He ran to her at once, and tried to take away her basket meaning to carry it for her.

She screamed at the top of her voice. 'Help! Help! He's robbing me! Help!'

Then up ran two men and Mr Plod the policeman. 'What are you doing to this old lady?' demanded Mr Plod. 'Oh, it's you, Meddle, is it? What sort of silly trick are you up to now?'

'I was about to do a good turn,' said Meddle haughtily. 'Can't I carry an old lady's basket for her if I want to?'

And off he went, feeling very angry, his nose in the air. He was most annoyed. All that fuss, and he had only wanted to carry a basket for somebody!

He walked down a long street. A woman came out of a gate with a dustbin and dumped it down by her gate, almost on Meddle's toe. He jumped and glared.

'Sorry,' said the woman. 'It's dustbin day. We all have to put our dustbins out for the dustmen to empty.'

'Dear, dear!' said Meddle. 'Do you mean to say you have to drag out those heavy dustbins all by yourself? That *is* a shame!'

'Oh, I don't mind for myself, I'm strong,' said the woman. 'But I'm sorry for old Mrs Lacy, who lives down the road there. Poor old thing, she finds it a heavy job.'

The woman went indoors and Meddle went on down the street. He thought he would offer to take out Mrs Lacy's dustbins for her. That would really be a good turn to do.

There was only one house that had no dustbins outside. That must be Mrs Lacy's, thought Meddle. Poor old thing – she hadn't been able to carry them out herself, and nobody else had offered to do so for her.

Well, he, Meddle, would do everything necessary!

He went in at the back way and had a look round. My, my, there were three big dustbins there – no wonder the poor old thing couldn't lift them. Meddle knocked at the back door to tell Mrs Lacy he was going to take her heavy dustbins out for her.

'Blim, blam!' he knocked, and waited. But nobody came to the door. 'Must be deaf,' thought Meddle, and knocked again. 'Old ladies often are, poor things.'

But even his much louder knocking didn't

bring Mrs Lacy to the door. Meddle looked at the dustbins. He could quite well take them out into the roadway now, and tell Mrs Lacy when she at last came to the door. Or maybe she was out and he could tell her when she came back.

So, with much puffing and panting, Meddle got one of the dustbins on to his back and staggered with it to the road. He set it down with a bang. Gracious, it was heavy!

Back he went for the second one, which was even heavier, and dumped that beside the first one. He mopped his forehead and panted. This really was a good deed! He felt quite exhausted already.

'Only one more,' thought Meddle and went back for it. He soon had that one beside the others, and then he saw that he was only just in time, because the dust-cart was coming down the street already.

'Ha! Just at the right moment,' said Mister Meddle, pleased. 'I'll wait here till the dustmen have emptied the three bins belonging to Mrs Lacy, and then I'll take them all back again. She *will* be so pleased! If it hadn't been for me coming along just at this moment, she wouldn't have had them stood outside, or emptied, or taken back to their place!'

He waited till the dustmen came along. They lifted the first bin up and emptied it into the cart. A terrific cloud of dust went up and everyone sneezed.

Then the second one was emptied, and then the third. Meddle trotted back with the empty dustbins, feeling very good and virtuous. He wished his Aunt Jemima could see him now. She would be sorry she had thought so unkindly of him.

He stood the dustbins in their places and knocked at the back door again. The next-door neighbour heard him and popped her head over the fence.

'No good knocking. They're out,' she said.

'Oh, well, never mind,' said Meddle, giving the woman a sweet smile, much to her surprise. 'I only wanted to say I'd taken out the full dustbins, and brought them back again when they were emptied. Good day!'

And with another sweet smile Meddle went up the path to the front, and was gone. He ambled down the road feeling very pleased with himself. He thought he wouldn't mind doing another good turn. But what? He came

to a gateway. Beside it stood a pot of white paint, and a brush stood in the pot. Nobody was about.

'The man must have gone in to his dinner,' thought Meddle looking at the gate. 'What was he doing? Oh – repainting the name of the house. Dear me, it so faint I can hardly read it.'

He bent to see what it was. It really was very faint indeed, and looked almost as if the painter had tried to take away the name before repainting it. Perhaps he wanted to do it differently this time, with bigger letters, thought Meddle.

'Fir Trees,' he read at last. He laughed. 'Well, well – isn't that just like some people! They call a house Fir Trees, and the only trees in the garden are rose bushes!'

He looked at the pot of paint. Wouldn't it be a very good turn if he painted the name again on the gate? The owner would be so pleased to come out from his dinner and find someone had done his work for him.

'I'm sure I could paint nicely,' thought Meddle picking up the paint-brush and looking at the white paint dripping off it on to the pavement below. 'It would be a nice job to do. Just the kind I like. Pity I haven't an overall or something, but I'll be careful not to mess my clothes.'

He began. He could just see the name 'Fir Trees' well enough to follow the letters over again with the white paint. He went over the line here and there, but he didn't notice that. He also dropped most of the paint on to the pavement and some on his coat and a good deal on his shoes, but he didn't notice that either.

'I'm doing another good deed,' said Meddle to himself. 'Really, Aunt Jemima has no right to scold me as she does. I can do more good deeds than she does. *She* would never have thought of taking out those dustbins, or of painting the name on this gate.'

Now, up the road, in the garden of the house whose dustbins Meddle had carried out to be emptied, quite a disturbance was going on. There was a lot of shouting and banging of dustbin lids, and the next-door neighbour popped her head over the fence to see whatever the matter was.

'Matter! Matter enough!' shouted a big, round, red-faced fellow with enormous black eyebrows. 'Someone's stolen the hen and pig food out of my bins! Look here – this is where the hen-feed was – and it's empty.' Bang! Down went a dustbin lid and another came up. 'And here's where the corn was and it's empty!' Bang! Down went that dustbin lid. 'And here's where the pig-food was, and it's empty!' Bang!

'Don't glare at me like that,' said the woman. '*I* haven't taken them. They've all been emptied into the dustman's cart.'

The red-faced man's eyebrows shot up till they almost disappeared. '*What*! Into the *dust-cart*! Say that again, Mrs Brown.'

She said it again, and then moved a little further away, afraid that her neighbour was going to burst with fury and rage.

'Who did that?' he spluttered at last. 'The dustmen? Did they dare to come and collect my dustbins? Why, they know I always burn my own rubbish and never want anything emptied!'

'No. It wasn't the dustmen,' said Mrs Brown. 'It was a funny-looking fellow with a long nose and untidy hair. He was banging at your back door to tell you he had taken out your bins to be emptied.'

The red-faced man could hardly believe this extraordinary tale. 'Where is this fellow?' he said at last.

'He went away,' said Mrs Brown. 'You might find him about the district if you go and look, though. You can't mistake his long nose – a real meddling nose it is, always being poked into somebody else's business, I should think.'

'It won't be poked into *mine* again,' said the red-faced man grimly, and he gritted his teeth together with a very nasty noise as he went to his front gate.

He walked down the road. Then he saw Meddle, who was still very busy painting the name on the gate. He had done as far as 'Fir Tre . .' and only had the letters *e* and *s* to do.

The red-faced man took a look at Meddle's long and pointed nose. Ha, there was no mistaking that! He tiptoed up behind him meaning to pounce on him unawares, but Meddle heard him gritting his teeth and looked round suddenly.

'GAAAAAAH!' yelled the man and flung himself on Meddle, who promptly sat down in the paint-pot and couldn't get out.

The brush flew up into the air and hit the

red-faced man over one eye. He stopped in surprise – and at that very moment out came the man who had been meaning to paint his gate and had gone in to his dinner.

He was very surprised to see one man sitting in his paint-pot and another man wiping white paint out of his eye.

'What's all this?' he cried angrily. 'Hey, get up out of my paint-pot, you! What are you doing here?'

'Sir,' said Meddle haughtily, trying to get up, but not being able to, 'sir, I was doing you a good turn. I was painting the name on your gate for you.'

The man looked at his gate and gave a howl of rage. 'What have you done that for? Fir Trees! You've gone and put "Fir Trees!"'

'Except for the last *e* and *s* I have,' said Meddle. 'That's what the name was, wasn't it? Though I must tell you I think it's a silly name because there are only rose bushes in your garden.'

'Well, what do you suppose I rubbed the name out for?' shouted the man. 'I was going to put "Rose-Cot" but I had to go in for my dinner. Now you've gone and put "Fir Trees" again. How dare you meddle? How dare you interfere? You come along in and I'll douse your head in cold water. I'll –'

'No, *I* want him,' said the red-faced man, and put his heavy hand on poor Meddle's shoulder. 'Do you know what he's done? He's gone and let the dustmen empty all my bins of hen-food and corn and pig-food into their cart! Grrrrrrrrr!'

He growled like a dog and shook Meddle

so hard that he came off the paint-pot, and rolled into the road. Both the men pounced on him at once, but the red-faced man put his foot into the paint-pot and fell over. The other man fell on top of him, and Meddle scrambled up quickly to rush away.

How he ran! He puffed and he panted, and ran till he felt he would burst. He sank down on a seat at a bus stop and buried his face in his hanky.

'Oh, dear! Two good turns gone west! How was I to know the silly fellow kept his hen-food in his dustbins? I thought old Mrs Lacy lived there. And how am I to know if people suddenly change their silly minds about the names of their silly houses? Rose-Cot! Ooooh, what a name!'

Now, who should come by to catch the next bus just then but his Aunt Jemima. Meddle saw her and moved up to give her room. He forgot that he had been sitting in a pot of white paint, and he had covered the seat with white patches. Before she could stop herself Aunt Jemima had sat down on a patch of wet paint. She leapt up again with a cry and craned her head over her back.

'Oh! My best black velvet skirt! You did that

on purpose, Meddle! You wicked fellow! Now you just come along home with me, and I'll show you what happens to people who put white paint on seats for me to sit on. A good scolding is what you need!'

Poor Meddle – if only he didn't meddle in other people's affairs he would get on much better, wouldn't he?

Chapter 6

Meddle in a Fog

'I'm going out to buy some sweets, Aunt Jemima,' said Meddle. 'Do you want any letters posted?'

'No, I don't. And you're not going out in this fog, Meddle,' said his aunt, firmly.

'What fog? Dear me, I hadn't noticed that it was foggy,' said Meddle, looking out of the window in surprise.

'No. You never notice things like that, unless it's pointed out to you,' said his aunt. 'The times you go out in the rain without your umbrella! The times you –'

Meddle scowled. If Aunt Jemima was going to scold him all afternoon he didn't want to stay in! Anyway, the fog wasn't very thick. It wouldn't in the least matter going out in it.

He got up. 'The fog's not too thick,' he said. 'I think I'll just go out and get my sweets, Aunt Jemima.'

'No. Sit down,' said his aunt. 'You know that old Mrs Trottle may be coming to tea this afternoon if it isn't too foggy – and I want you to change into your clean suit, and wash your dirty hands and brush your hair. Otherwise you certainly can't come and have tea with us – and that means you won't have any cake or jam sandwich.'

'Oooh – is there to be a special tea?' said Meddle, who was greedy. 'All right, I'll go and change now, and get as clean as I can.'

But he didn't go upstairs to change. He tip-toed to the back door and let himself out! 'I'm going to get my sweets, whatever mean old Aunt Jemima says!' he thought. '*I* shan't get lost in the fog! Aunt will never know, because she will think I am upstairs changing my clothes and washing myself!'

And out into the fog he went. It wasn't too bad, really. He could see about three yards in front of him, and he made his way to the sweet shop quite easily. He bought his sweets and then went to look round the pet shop next door. It was a good thing he had no more money to spend or he would have bought a black dog, a white cat, two mice and a parrot that would say 'Pass the salt, please,' and then cackle loudly just like a hen that has laid an egg. Meddle thought it was wonderful.

When he got out of the pet shop the fog was much thicker. Oh, dear – he could hardly see his way at all now! He groped down the street, feeling the railings at one side.

He got to the corner and went round it. Then he wondered if it was the wrong corner. He looked at the names on the gates. Oh, dear – he didn't know them at all!

'Cosy-Cot! Why, that's not a house near us,' he said to himself! 'And here's Green Gates – I never remember seeing that in my life! I'd better go back to the corner.'

So he did, and crossed the road there and went over to the other side. 'This must be right now,' he thought. 'Now – down this road, round the corner, turn to the left, and there I shall be, at home! I shall creep in at the back door, go upstairs to wash and change – and Aunt Jemima will never, never know I've been out. Wouldn't I get a scolding if she did!'

But he didn't come to his aunt's house. He stopped in despair. 'I must be lost! This fog's so thick, now, I can hardly see. And it's getting dark, too. Bother! What shall I do?'

He went a little further on, hoping to meet someone and ask the way. But he didn't meet anyone at all. He stood still and frowned.

Was he anywhere near his home at all? He *must* find it because if he didn't Aunt Jemima would send out a search party for him, and would be so cross when he was found and brought back. Besides he would miss that lovely tea if he wasn't quick!

He thought of the tea. Chocolate cake with cream in the middle – jam sandwich that melted in his mouth – and perhaps some of those shortbread biscuits that Aunt Jemima made so well. He set off walking again.

But still he couldn't find out where he was. And now it really was getting darker. 'I'll have to go in at a gate, knock on a front door, and ask how to get to my own home,' thought Meddle at last. So he went in at the nearest gate, marched up the path and banged on the front door.

Footsteps came down the hall, which was

dark. The door opened and someone peered out.

'Please,' said Meddle, 'I'm lost in the fog. I want to get home quickly because my aunt is having a very nice tea – so could you tell me where I live?'

'Yes,' said the person at the door, 'you live here!'

A ıd Meddle was dragged indoors and the door was slammed shut. It was his Aunt Jemima speaking to him! He had chosen his very own house to come and ask at for help! Well, well, well – how exactly like poor old Meddle!

'Oh, Aunt Jemima – oh dear – you see I just slipped out for a minute, and . . .' stammered Meddle, but after giving him a very hard stare, Aunt Jemima disappeared into the sitting room and shut the door. Meddle heard the sound of voices.

He remembered the lovely tea. He shot upstairs. He was very dirty and untidy. It took him a long time to get himself clean, brush his hair down well, and change into his other clothes.

'Now I'll go down,' he said, looking at himself in the glass. 'I look very neat and nice. I can hear Mrs Trottle is still downstairs – Aunt won't say anything nasty to me in front of her, and I'll soon tuck into the cakes.'

So down he went, practising a polite party smile, as he trotted down the stairs. He opened the door and walked in, bowing politely to old Mrs Trottle, and asking her how she was.

'Oh – there you are at last, Meddle,' said his aunt. 'Well, all the tea-things are stacked up in the kitchen, ready for you to wash. You can go and do them now!'

Well, well, well – what a shock for Meddle. He found himself out in the cold kitchen, faced by an enormous pile of dirty cups and saucers and knives and spoons and plates and dishes! He scowled.

'I'll jolly well tuck into the cakes first,' he said. But he couldn't! Aunt Jemima had put them away and locked the cupboard door.

And will you believe it, when he had washed up and went upstairs gloomily to fetch his sweets to eat, his aunt's old dog had been there first! Not a sweet was left in the bag.

But Aunt Jemima wouldn't scold the dog. 'All these things have happened because you were stupid and disobedient, Meddle,' she said. 'In fact, the only clever thing you did was to pick your own house to come to when you were lost.'

'It wasn't clever,' said poor Meddle, feeling very miserable indeed. 'It was just about the silliest thing I could have done. And if ever I lose myself in a fog again I'll be jolly careful I don't get lost exactly outside my own house!'

Chapter 7

Meddle and the Biggle-Gobble

'Meddle, for goodness' sake, go out for a walk and stop meddling in my cooking,' said Aunt Jemima, crossly. 'You've put salt in the pie instead of sugar, and dropped all the currants on the floor, and –'

'All right, Aunt, all right. No need to get cross just because I'm helping,' said Meddle, and he reached for his hat. He had just spilt the custard powder, and he thought he had better go out before his aunt discovered that, too. Dear, dear – what a pity people wouldn't let him be kind and help them more!

Meddle had one of his interfering moods on when he felt he could do things very much better than anyone else. He wondered if he should call at the butcher's and tell him how to make bigger sausages. He decided he wouldn't because the butcher had a nasty-looking chopper and might chase him.

'I might, perhaps, go in and tell the baker how to make a much, much richer fruit cake by putting in twice as many raisins and currants,' he said, but when he peeped in at the baker's shop window he saw that Mrs Biscuit, the baker's wife, was at the counter that day, instead of the kindly baker himself.

'She's quite likely to throw hard, stale buns at me if I try to help her,' thought Meddle. 'And, what's more, she'd probably hit me every time. No – I won't help the baker today.'

He walked on till he came to Dame Rimminy's cottage. He saw green smoke coming from her chimney, so he knew she was making spells that morning. Ah, now – if he could help *her*, how grateful she would be! He walked up to the door.

It was wide open. Meddle looked inside. There was a small round room, and in the middle of it was a peculiar fire with green flames. On it hung a black pot out of which green smoke came. Dame Rimminy was making a really fine spell, no doubt about that!

Meddle looked for her. She wasn't there. She was at the bottom of her garden looking for the very earliest snowdrop, which she wanted for her spell.

Meddle tiptoed to the pot. My, my – how it gurgled and bubbled! What spell was Dame Rimminy making?

He caught sight of a big, black book on a nearby table – 'The Big Book of Useful Spells'. Meddle read its title and then looked at the page where the book was opened.

'Ha – A Spell for Making a Biggle-Gobble,' he read out loud. 'Dear me – a *Biggle-Gobble*. What *can* that be? I've never heard of such a thing before. How very, very exciting!'

He read the directions: 'Get the pot boiling till the smoke is green. Now put in one cat's hair, half a spoonful of rice dipped in red ink, one old shoe, two pinches of Glory Powder, and stir with a feathered hat. Chant the following three times, and then wait five minutes for the Biggle-Gobble to appear.'

Meddle smiled happily. Why – he could do all that easily! Perhaps if he made the Biggle-Gobble, whatever it was, for Dame Rimminy, she would be so pleased with him that she would give him one of her famous Magic Toffees. You put one in your mouth, and, however much you sucked it, you could never, never suck it all away. Meddle had always longed for a Magic Toffee.

He began to make the spell. 'One cat's hair. Come here, Puss. Now, keep still, I only want *one* hair. I'm going to pull. Oh, you naughty cat, you scratched me!'

So she had – but Meddle had some hairs. He dropped one into the pot. Then he found a tin labelled '*Rice*' and took out half a spoonful. He found the bottle of red ink in Dame Rimminy's desk, and poured it over the rice. It went bright red immediately.

'Into the pot with you!' said Meddle, and into the pot went the rice dyed red! The pot gave a sudden gurgle and made Meddle jump. He peered into it. Was the Biggle-Gobble forming already?

'Now to put in one old shoe,' he said, and he looked for one. He saw two shoes belonging to Dame Rimminy standing on the floor. He looked at them. 'Well – they're not new, so I suppose they might be called *old*,' he said.

He picked one up and flung it into the bubbling pot. It almost bubbled over, and a strange snorting noise began to come out of it. Meddle felt rather alarmed. Still – he must certainly go on with the spell now. It was very, very bad to begin a spell and not to finish it.

'Now for two pinches of Glory-Powder,' said Meddle, and looked all round for it. Ah – there it was, in a tin on the top shelf. He climbed up and got it. He scattered two pinches of the curious yellow powder into the pot.

It jerked and bubbled and snorted as if

something alive was in it. Meddle felt quite excited. 'Now I must stir it with a feathered hat and chant the magic words!' he said.

He looked about and saw a fine feathered hat belonging to Dame Rimminy hanging on a peg. Ah! – that was just the thing.

He took it and began to stir the bubbling pot with it, chanting the magic words: 'Chirimmy, chuckadee, lillity-loo, Come Biggle-Gobble, I'm waiting for you. Chirimmy, chuckadee, lillity-loo!'

He threw the wet-feathered hat on the floor and waited. Five minutes more and the Biggle-Gobble would appear! Whatever would it be like? Wouldn't Dame Rimminy be pleased to see that he had made the spell for her!

But at that very moment Dame Rimminy came in with a small snowdrop. She glared at Meddle.

'What are *you* here for? You know I don't like anyone here when I'm making a spell. Get out!'

'Oh, but Dame Rimminy – I've been saving you a lot of trouble,' said Meddle, smiling. '*I've* made your spell for you. It will soon be ready!'

'Nonsense!' said Dame Rimminy. 'No one can make a Flyaway Spell except me!'

'A – a *Flyaway* Spell, did you say?' said Meddle, puzzled. 'But – but I thought you were making a Biggle-Gobble spell!'

'Don't be silly. Who wants a Biggle-Gobble?' said Dame Rimminy.

'Your book was open at that spell,' said poor Meddle. Dame Rimminy stepped over to it. She turned over the page and showed Meddle what was printed there, 'How to Make a Flyaway Spell.'

'The wind blew the page over, that's all,' she said. 'I wasn't going to make a Biggle-Gobble spell. Whatever *would* I do with a hungry Biggle-Gobble!'

'Are they hungry?' said Meddle, edging towards the door, and watching the bubbling pot with great alarm.

'Always hungry,' said Dame Rimminy. Then she caught sight of her feathered hat lying in a puddle on the floor. She pounced on it.

'Meddle! MEDDLE! You haven't been using my best hat to stir the pot with, have you? And where is my other shoe? Have you thrown that in the pot? Come here, Meddle. Stand still and answer me or I'll

scold you from now until tomorrow. Come *here*, Meddle!'

But Meddle was tearing round and round the room, trying to get away from the angry old dame. And all the time the pot kept bubbling and gurgling and snorting. Three minutes had gone – four minutes – FIVE MINUTES!

BANG! CRASH! SNORT!

Out of the pot leapt a Biggle-Gobble. Meddle stared at it in the greatest alarm. It was rather like a small dragon, with a round head like a cat's, and long ears – and far, far

75

too many teeth! It stood and snorted in the middle of the floor.

'After him, Biggle-Gobble!' shouted Dame Rimminy. 'After him! If you're hungry, he's the one to catch!'

Meddle gave a loud yell and leapt straight out of the window. The Biggle-Gobble leapt out too. And then, my word, what a wonderful chase there was! Down the garden and over the wall, along the street and round the corner, over the stile and across the field,

into the lane and up the hill, along the High Street and helter-skelter for Meddle's Aunt Jemima!

The Biggle-Gobble thoroughly enjoyed it. But Meddle didn't. His heart beat so fast and he panted so loudly that he really frightened himself. Why, oh, why, had he meddled in that spell, and made a Biggle-Gobble!

He rushed into his aunt's house – but before he could bang on the door the Biggle-Gobble was in the hall too. Aunt Jemima heard the noise and came out of the kitchen in surprise. When she saw the Biggle-Gobble she gave a shriek.

'A Biggle-Gobble! How *dare* you bring one home, Meddle! It'll eat everything! They're always hungry!'

'Don't let it eat me, don't let it,' wailed Meddle, and dived behind the sofa.

'Where did it come from?' demanded Aunt Jemima, flapping at the Biggle-Gobble with a newspaper, just as if it were a wasp.

'From Dame Rimminy's,' sobbed poor Meddle.

'I'll telephone her at once and tell her to come and take it away,' said Aunt Jemima. 'Oh, my goodness, it's eating up all my new cakes. Shoo, you greedy creature, shoo!'

She went to the telephone and rang up Dame Rimminy. 'What do you want to go making Biggle-Gobbles for? One has chased Meddle home and it's eating my cakes. *What's* that you say? *Meddle* made it? It's his Biggle-Gobble, and he can keep it? But, I tell you, it's in my house and won't go away. I *won't* keep it!'

She slammed down the telephone receiver and glared at the Biggle-Gobble, who was now eating a pie. 'Stop that!' she shouted. 'Go and nibble Meddle's toes. Go and nibble his red ears.'

'No, no, Aunt,' wailed Meddle, and fled out of the door in fright. The Biggle-Gobble followed him at once. Aunt Jemima shut the door with a bang and bolted it. Then she fastened all the windows. Meddle could play about with the Biggle-Gobble all he liked – it wasn't coming back *here*!

The Biggle-Gobble gave Meddle a nip with its sharp teeth, but it didn't like the taste of him. So it trotted off to somebody's dustbin, took the lid off and began to gobble up potato peel. Meddle slid round the corner and ran off at top speed.

He went back to his aunt's at sixty miles an hour, climbed up the tree outside his window, and broke the glass to get in. His Aunt Jemima was very angry, and chased him up and down stairs just like the Biggle-Gobble – except that she had a very nasty walking stick in her hand.

Poor Meddle. He's afraid to go out of the house in case he meets the Biggle-Gobble, so he's got to stay indoors and scrub and wash and polish till his arms are ready to drop off.

'I'll never meddle with spells again,' he says. 'That awful Biggle-Gobble! I do hope it isn't still waiting for me round the corner.'

It isn't. It went back to Dame Rimminy and she gave it a good meal of dog biscuits and milk, and it curled up by the fire and went to sleep, purring. She sold it to the Green Witch for three golden pounds, because the witch had too many mice and the Biggle-Gobble was really a wonderful mouser.

But, Meddle doesn't know that. He thinks it's still looking for him!

Chapter 8

Meddle Goes Shopping

One day Meddle went to see his Aunt Jemima. He had been keeping away from her for some time because she wasn't at all pleased with his meddling ways.

He found a note on the back door.

'Baker. One loaf, please.'

'Milkman. One pint, please.'

'Laundry. Look in scullery.'

'Dear me!' thought Meddle. 'Aunt Jemima must be out, or else she's ill in bed. I'll go in and see.'

So he pushed open the kitchen door and in he went. No one seemed to be about. Meddle went to the larder door and opened it. Ooooh! Jam tarts on a plate. He was just about to take one when a voice made him jump.

'If that's the baker, leave a cake, too!'

'It isn't the baker. It's me, Meddle,' called Meddle. 'Where are you, Aunt Jemima?'

'I've got a chill and I'm in bed,' said the voice, rather croakily. 'Come up and see me. And DON'T snoop round the larder, Meddle. I know exactly how many jam tarts there are.'

Meddle frowned, shut the larder door softly, and went upstairs. His aunt was in bed with an enormous night-cap on, and a great array of medicine bottles by her side.

'Poor Aunt Jemima! Can I do anything for you?' asked Meddle. 'Shall I give you your medicine? You do look ill.'

'I feel it,' groaned his aunt. 'Yes, give me my medicine. It's in the blue bottle.'

Meddle got the bottle. 'How much do I pour you?' he asked.

'A tablespoonful,' said his aunt, lying with her eyes shut, looking very miserable indeed. Meddle poured out the medicine into a tablespoon. Then he held it out. 'Sit up, Aunt Jemima. Here's your medicine.'

She sat up, and Meddle held the spoon to her mouth. But as soon as she tasted it she gave a loud yell and knocked the spoon out of Meddle's hand. The medicine went all over him.

'Meddle! What's that? That isn't my nice, sweet cough medicine. It's HORRIBLE!'

'Well, you said the blue bottle,' said Meddle, holding it up. His aunt groaned, and lay down again.

'That's my eye-drops. You would get the wrong bottle! Couldn't you even look to see what the label says as plain as can be – *eye-drops*.'

'I'm sorry, Aunt,' said Meddle, picking up

another blue bottle. 'I'll give you the right medicine this time.'

'No, you won't. You won't give me anything at all, if I can help it,' said his aunt. 'All I want you to do is to go away as quickly as possible before you start meddling. Go home, Meddle, go home!'

'You sound as if I were a dog!' said Meddle indignantly. 'Please, Aunt, isn't there anything I can do? Don't you want any shopping done, for instance?'

'Yes, I do,' said his aunt, shutting her eyes again. 'But *you're* not going to do it, Meddle! I know what your shopping is like. Even if you take a list with you you always bring the wrong things back. Meddle and muddle, that's what you do! Go home!'

Meddle was very hurt. He went down the stairs and into the scullery. A voice followed him. 'And don't forget that the larder door squeaks, Meddle! I know when anyone is opening it!'

Meddle thought his aunt was being unfair. He wished he could show her she was wrong about him. Didn't he want to be helpful? Yes, he did! Then why wouldn't she let him at least do her shopping?

His eye caught sight of a list on the kitchen table. Ah! This must be Aunt Jemima's shopping list. Maybe she had just been going out shopping when she had fallen ill. Well, what about Mister Meddle taking the list, doing the shopping simply beautifully, and showing his Aunt Jemima that he really was a clever fellow after all?

He put his hand into his pocket. Had he got any money with him that morning? Yes, he had. His uncle had sent him quite a lot for his birthday the week before. Should he go shopping with his own money and get it back from his aunt afterwards – or should he go back upstairs and ask her for some shopping money?

'No. She wouldn't give me any – and she would still say I wasn't to do the shopping,' said Meddle to himself. 'I'll use my own – and when I come back with all the things on the list, she'll be so pleased with me that she'll give me a few extra pence for my trouble, as well as the money I have spent.'

He picked up the neat little list and went out of the house. He looked at the list as he went.

One small blue tablecloth. Well, that's easy.

I know just the kind she has! One tea-cloth.
That's easy too, I can get it at the same
shop. One white apron. Lucky I know the
kind she wears in the morning! I'll have to
get a nice big size for Aunt Jemima because
she's rather fat. I'll go to the draper's for all
these.'

He looked at the list again. 'One sheet.
One pillowcase. One Turkish towel, small.
Well, well – this is really quite a bit of luck. I
can do all the shopping at the same shop! I'm
sure the draper will sell all these.'

Meddle was pleased. This was very easy

86

shopping to do. He hoped he had enough money.

He went to the draper's and walked to the counter that sold towels and sheets and pillowcases.

'I want a nice white sheet, please, for a single bed, and a pillowcase to match, and a small Turkish towel,' said Meddle.

'Only *one* sheet, sir? asked the shop girl. 'We usually sell them in pairs.'

'Well, my aunt only wants *one*,' said Meddle, firmly. 'So one it must be.'

The shop girl managed to find an odd sheet, a plain pillowcase and a small Turkish towel.

'Anything else?' she asked.

'Oh, yes. One small blue tablecloth, one tea-cloth and a white apron, large size,' said Meddle, looking at his list. 'That's all. I'll take them with me.'

He had them wrapped up, and the girl gave him the bill. Oh dear – it took nearly all the money his uncle had sent him for his birthday. Never mind – Aunt Jemima would repay it all.

He went out of the shop, pleased with himself. Now Aunt Jemima would see how clever he could be at shopping! He was sure that he had got just the right things.

He went back to the house and let himself in at the back door.

Somebody else was there, too – the young man from the laundry. He was collecting the basket of washing.

'Good morning,' he said to Meddle. 'I've come for the laundry – but I can't find the washing list. Have you seen it?'

'No, I haven't,' said Meddle. The young man went to the bottom of the stairs and called loudly.

'Your nephew is here, Ma'am, and *he* can't find the washing list either. So I'll just take the washing without it, and make out a list for you myself.'

'Thank you,' called back Aunt Jemima, croakily. The young man went out and shut the door, carrying the basket on his shoulder. Meddle ran upstairs with his parcel, beaming all over his face.

'Aunt Jemima, I found your shopping list and I've been shopping for you! Look!'

'What *do* you mean?' said his aunt, amazed. Meddle undid the parcel in great haste, anxious to show all the things he had bought.

'One sheet. One tablecloth, blue. One apron. One tea-cloth. One Turkish towel. One pillowcase. There you are – and here's the bill. Now, don't say I make a muddle whenever I go shopping!'

Aunt Jemima stared at the things in astonishment. 'But why did you buy all these?' she said. 'I don't wan them!'

'Well, they were on your shopping list downstairs!' said Meddle, and he pushed the list into his aunt's hands. 'See – they're all down there.'

'Meddle,' said his aunt, 'Meddle, are you *quite* mad? This is the *laundry* list – the list of things I was sending to be washed. No wonder the man couldn't find it. Is there any sense in taking a *washing* list and going out to *buy* all the things on it?'

'Oh, Aunt – I thought it was your shopping list!' wailed Meddle. 'I did really. Please pay me back for all I've bought.'

'Certainly not,' said his aunt. 'Take them home yourself and use them – and tie the apron round your waist when you do your washing-up! You'll look fine! Go home, Meddle. If you don't, I'll get up and take the broom to you!'

So now Meddle is going home with all the things he bought, because the shop won't take them back. He's very sad – he has wasted his money, and made such a muddle again. He never *will* learn not to meddle, will he?

Chapter 9

A Surprise for Mister Meddle

Mister Meddle was always meddling in things that were no business of his, and poking his nose in where he wasn't wanted.

But he got a great surprise when he went to stay with his cousins, Snip and Snap. They didn't like meddlers, they didn't like borrowers, and they got very impatient indeed with their cousin Meddle.

'Who's taken my new whipping-top?' said Snip. 'You, Meddle? Well, where is it then? Where have you put it?'

'Dear me – I'm sure I put it back on the shelf,' said Meddle. But it wasn't there, of course.

'Meddle! Did you borrow my watch?' asked Snap. 'I can't find it anywhere.'

'Dear me – yes, I did,' said Meddle, looking at his wrist. 'I wanted to be sure of catching my bus, you know. Oh, Snap – I'm sorry, but it must have slipped off my wrist.'

'Meddle, did you go and give the cat that milk pudding out of the larder?' called his Aunt Amanda. 'Or did you eat it yourself?'

'Oh, Aunt, the cat mewed so loudly and was so hungry I thought you'd *want* me to give it

something to eat,' said Meddle. 'And I don't much like milk pudding.'

'Well, other people do,' said his aunt crossly. 'Snip and Snap – you'll have to deal with Meddle for me. If he meddles much more I'll send him away!'

'If you take our things again and lose them or don't bring them back we'll use magic on *your* things – and we'll make them disappear!' said Snip to Meddle.

'Pooh!' said Meddle. 'You're only kids. You don't know any magic. You ought to be *pleased* when I bother myself with your things.'

'Well, we're not,' said Snap. 'Now remember, Meddle – the very next time you meddle with our things, we shall meddle with yours – and away they'll go under your very nose!'

Meddle didn't believe Snip and Snap. He took no notice of their threats at all. He just went on doing what he liked. He borrowed their ball to play with and it fell into a gutter on the roof of the house and couldn't be got down. He borrowed Snap's new socks and because they were too small he wore them into holes.

'He's hopeless,' said Snip to Snap. 'We'll have to teach him a lesson. What about our wonderful Disappearing Trick?'

'Oooh, yes,' said Snap. 'We'll get our friends in to help. Let's call a meeting. We'll ask Tippy, Jinky, Impy and Heyho.'

So all those four met with Snip and Snap at Tippy's and talked about how to punish Meddle for his aggravating ways.

'We'll do the Disappearing Trick on him,' said Snip. 'We'll get his football, his cricket bat, his new pair of socks and his football boots. We'll tie long, long black thread to them, and tie the other ends to your bicycles.'

Snap began to giggle as he saw the surprised faces of the others.

'It's all right, we're not mad,' he said. 'It's a trick we've played before. Now you, Tippy, can have the socks tied to your bicycle. The black thread will be very long indeed, and won't be seen – so a long time after you've passed by on your bicycle the socks will come dragging along the road, looking as if they're coming all by themselves. You'll be out of sight, you see!'

Tippy laughed loudly. 'My, what a good trick! And I suppose you'll tie the other things to the other bicycles, and they'll come along the road, too!'

'Yes – we'll tie the boots to Jinky's bicycle, the football to Impy's and the cricket bat to Heyho's,' grinned Snip. 'You'll ride by one after another, you see, and Meddle won't *dream* that anything is tied to you. The socks will come wriggling along like snakes, the boots will come jiggling by, the football will bounce along all by itself and the cricket bat will race along like anything.'

Everyone began to laugh. Impy held his sides. 'My, this is the best joke I've ever heard of. When do we play it?'

'This evening,' said Snap. 'We'll get you the socks and all the other things this afternoon when Meddle is out, and we'll give you reels of black thread, too. You can each tie your things on, and then go to the little shed at the end of Jiminy Lane.'

'You'll see us walking by with Meddle,' said Snip. 'And that will be your signal to set out – one by one, mind, with about a minute's time between each. Leave us to do the rest!'

'I shall fall off my bicycle with laughing,' said Impy. 'I know I shall.'

'I'd love to see Meddle's face when his

football comes bouncing by on its own!' said Jinky.

Everyone went home, giggling. What a trick! Whatever would Meddle say?

Now, that evening, when everything was ready and prepared, Snip and Snap went to Meddle.

'Have you found my watch?' demanded Snap.

'What about my ball?' said Snip.

'Oh, go away,' said Meddle, crossly. 'You

know I haven't found them. Leave me alone. I'm going for my evening walk and I don't want you.'

But Snip and Snap went with him. They went down the lane, and passed the little shed. Inside were Tippy, Jinky, Impy and Heyho waiting impatiently with their bicycles. Tied to the backs of them with long black thread were all the things belonging to Meddle!

'Meddle, we're going to teach you a lesson,' said Snip, solemnly. 'We're going to work some magic here tonight, and send away some of the things you like best – things belonging to *you*!'

'Oh, don't be silly,' said Meddle. 'Go home! As if *you* knew any magic!'

'Meddle,' said Snap, in such a peculiar voice that Meddle stopped, startled. 'Meddle! Would you like to see your new socks, your football boots, your football and your cricket bat all disappear?'

'Don't talk nonsense,' said Meddle uneasily. 'And let me tell you that if you take them from my room and hide them, I'll tell your mother!'

'Oh, we won't hide them!' said Snip. 'We'll

call them from your room this very minute –
and we'll send them rushing up the road as
fast as can be – off to the Land of Rubbish, as
sure as eggs are eggs!'

'I don't believe a word of it,' said Meddle,
scornfully. 'If I *see* my socks rushing by, I'll
believe it, certainly – but not until. Magic like
that isn't learnt by kids like you!'

A bicycle came down the lane. Tippy was
riding it. Snip and Snap didn't smile at him,
and he didn't wave to them. Meddle didn't
know him.

'Just wait till this bicycle's gone by,' said
Snip. 'Ah, he's gone. Now then – SOCKS,
COME BY AND RUN AWAY!'

Something black and wriggly now
appeared a little way down the road. It was
Meddle's socks, tied to the distant bicycle
with long black thread. The thread couldn't
be seen – but here came the socks, wriggling
along fast like excited black snakes!

They passed in half a moment, and Meddle
clutched at Snip and Snap in horror.

'Oooh! I say they *did* look like my socks!
Snip, is it magic? Snap, don't do this. I don't
like it. Were those really my socks?'

'Of course,' said Snip, trying not to laugh.

He saw the next bicycle coming, with Jinky in the saddle. He nudged Snap.

'And now I think we'll call for Meddle's football boots to come!' said Snap. 'BOOTS, COME BY AND RUN AWAY!'

Jinky had gone by on his bicycle, grinning, but not looking at Snip or Snap. Meddle looked down the road in alarm. What was this jigging along? Could it be – could it *really* be – his football boots?

'It is, it is! It's my boots!' cried poor Meddle, looking quite pale. 'Oh, stop, boots! Stop! There they go, my lovely boots!'

And there they went, jigging along the road on the black thread, Jinky's distant bicycle pulling them fast. They looked most peculiar.

'Snip! Snap! Don't do any more magic,' wailed Meddle. 'I don't like it. It's horrible. I've lost my socks and now my boots.'

Impy came by on his bicycle next, pedalling fast, afraid that he might explode into laughter at the sight of Meddle's face. Snip called out, as soon as he had gone by:

'FOOTBALL, COME BY AND RUN AWAY!'

'No, no!' begged Meddle. 'Not my football. Not my fine, splendid football! Oh, my, oh, my – it's coming! It's coming, as sure as anything! And I daren't stop it, I daren't. I'm afraid I might go off to the Land of Rubbish, too!'

Snip and Snap turned away to laugh. The football bounced along like a live thing, leaping high in the air if it touched a stone or a rut. It went by at top speed, and Meddle sat down on the kerb and groaned.

'Snip and Snap, I'll never meddle with your things again, never. Please, please, stop this. I'm frightened. I'm very – oh, my goodness me, is this something else coming?'

Heyho had cycled by, and behind him at a good distance came the cricket bat, sliding along fairly smoothly, but giving little jigs when it passed over a stone. Snip giggled. Meddle covered his face with his hands as soon as he heard Snap shouting to the bat to come by and run away.

'There goes my wonderful bat! Is there no end to this? Snip, forgive me. Now that I see my own treasures rushing off to the Land of Rubbish I know how you must have felt when I lost your ball and your watch and spoilt your socks, and gave your pudding to the cat, and –'

'All right. We'll stop the magic now,' said

Snip, with another giggle. 'We did think of sending your trunk off, too, but we thought we'd better not, or you might live with us the rest of your life if you'd no trunk to pack to go away.'

'I'm going away,' said Meddle. 'I'm leaving you tomorrow. You're too magic for me! I'd be afraid of ever borrowing anything again. And do you know what I'm going to do before I go?'

'No. What?' asked Snip and Snap.

'I'm going to get some money out of my bank,' said Meddle, 'and I'm going to buy a

new watch and a new ball, and new socks for
you, and all the things I've ever borrowed
and lost I'll buy and give you. This has been a
lesson to me. My goodness – how magic you
are!'

Snip and Snap were surprised to hear all
this. They looked at one another, feeling
rather awkward.

'Well, if you really are sorry – and will really
buy us all the things you've borrowed and
spoilt and lost – maybe we'll use our magic to

102

get back the things of yours that have rushed by this evening, and disappeared,' said Snip.

Meddle beamed. 'Will you really? That's grand of you! I'm afraid of going to the Land of Rubbish to fetch them.'

'Yes. They might keep you there,' said Snap, and giggled. 'All right, Meddle, it's a bargain – you buy us new things in place of the ones you've lost or spoilt and we'll get all *your* things back for you!'

Well, of course, it was easy to get them back, as you can imagine! They just went round to Tippy's the next day, and found Tippy, Jinky, Impy and Heyho there with all the things quite safe – and what a laugh they had together when they remembered how everything had rushed by the night before!

Meddle went out that morning, got some money and bought a whole lot of new things. He gave them to Snip and Snap and his Aunt Amanda. He packed his trunk. He sent a note to the station to ask a porter to fetch it. He really seemed quite a different person!

He was very glad to have his socks, boots, ball and bat back. He looked at Snip and Snap in awe and admiration.

'I never knew you were so magic,' he said.

'You frighten me! My word, I'm going to be careful in future!'

He said goodbye and off he went, swinging his stick in the air.

'I say,' said Snip, suddenly. 'Meddle lost his stick last week. Whose stick was that? It wasn't our *very best one*, was it?'

They rushed to the hall-stand to see if their stick was there. It was gone. Their mother called out to them.

'Meddle has borrowed it. He says he'll send it back next week.'

But will he? Snip and Snap can't make up their minds if he will or not – and neither can I! *What* a joke they played on Meddle, didn't they? I wish I'd been there to see it.

Chapter 10

Goodbye, Mister Meddle

Mister Meddle always liked roaming round the railway station. It was a most exciting place, with trains puffing in and out, people hurrying all about, and porters shouting, 'Mind your backs, please!'

One morning he went into the station, and sat down on a seat to watch what was going on. He saw the people buying their tickets, carrying their luggage, looking for their trains.

'They all look very worried,' said Meddle to himself. 'Very worried indeed. Perhaps I'd better help some of them.'

Now, Meddle, as you know, was exactly like his name. If he could poke his long nose into anything and meddle with it, he was happy! So up he got to see what he could do.

He met a little man panting and puffing, carrying a very heavy bag. Meddle went up to him and tried to get hold of it. 'Let me help,' he said.

'Certainly not. Let go,' said the man, fiercely. 'I know what you'd do if I let you take my bag – run off with it! And that's the last I would see of it.'

'What a dreadful thing to say!' said Meddle, and stalked off crossly. He bumped into a woman who was carrying three parcels and dragging a little dog along too. 'Allow me, Madam!' said Meddle politely, and took the biggest parcel from the woman.

The dog immediately flew at him and nipped his leg. Meddle dropped the parcel and howled. There was crash!

'There now!' said the woman, angrily. 'I had my best glass bowls packed in that parcel! What do you think you are doing, snatching it from me?'

'Your horrible dog bit me,' said Meddle, most annoyed.

'Well, of course he did!' said the woman. 'He thought you were stealing my parcel. It served you right. Please call a porter and ask him to clear up this mess of broken glass –

and you will have to pay me five pounds for breaking the bowls.'

A porter came up. 'I saw you meddling!' he said to Meddle. 'If parcels want carrying, *I'll* carry them. It's my job, not yours. And *you* can clear up the mess, because that's your job, not mine!'

Well, you would have thought that Meddle would have had enough of poking his nose into other people's affairs by then, wouldn't you? Not a bit of it! He paid the angry woman five pounds, he cleared up the mess – and then he went around looking for somebody else to meddle with.

He saw a little man, a big, plump woman, and four children all trailing along. 'Oh dear, oh dear!' said the woman. 'We shall miss the train, I know! Where do we get our tickets?'

'Madam, over there,' said Meddle, hurrying up to her. 'Shall I hold the children's hands while you get them?'

'No, thank you,' said the woman. 'They can hold each other's hands. Dad, get your money ready for the tickets. Oh dear, what a queue there is at the ticket office!'

'Madam, you go and get your seats in the train and I'll buy the tickets for you,' said Meddle.

'Do go away!' said the little man, crossly. 'I'm not leaving you here with my money, I wouldn't be so silly!'

'That's not a nice thing to say at all!' said Meddle, most offended. 'Do you mean to say I'd run off with the money? Well, I never heard such a –'

'Do please go away,' said the plump woman. 'We can look after ourselves all right. Oh my, oh my, what a queue. I wish these people in front of us would hurry up, I know we shall miss our train.'

'We'll catch it all right,' said the little man,

looking at the station clock. 'But if its crowded we shan't get any seats, that's certain.'

The children began to cry. 'I want a seat,' sobbed one. 'I want to look out of the window.'

'Shall I go and get some seats for you?' said Meddle, quite determined to help in some way. 'I could go and find a carriage and put newspapers and things on six seats – then no one would take those seats, and when you came along you could have them. I could hop out of the carriage and wave goodbye.'

'What an extraordinary fellow!' said the little man to his wife. He turned to Meddle. 'I tell you, we don't want people poking their noses into our business,' he said. 'We can't stop you finding seats, of course, and spreading them with newspapers and coats to keep them for us! I can see you mean to interfere with us in *some* way!'

'Not interfere – just *help*,' said Meddle, quite hurt. 'All right – I'm off to get some seats for you. I'll buy some newspapers to spread on them, so that people will know they are all reserved for others!'

He turned away, pleased. He bought some

papers and then ran to find the train. Bother!
He had forgotten to ask which one it was. It
must be the very next train leaving, because
the little man and his wife were in such a
hurry to get the tickets. One of the children
had said they were going to the sea – now
which train would it be?

'Ah – here's one leaving in five minutes – to
Seaside Town,' said Meddle. 'This must be it.
How glad they will be when they come
rushing on to the platform, find the train is
full – but with six seats saved for them!'

He bought a platform ticket and hurried to
the train. He found a carriage that was quite
empty. Good! He sat down, and arranged

four newspapers and his overcoat on five
seats. He sat in the sixth himself, of course.

He felt pleased with himself. 'It's so nice to
help people,' he said. 'Now that little family
will all travel comfortably to the seaside, each
with a nice seat all the way.'

People looked into the carriage, saw the
newspapers and coat on the seats and went
on again. Meddle grinned. Aha! He had been
very clever, he thought.

The minutes went by. Meddle began to feel
anxious. Surely those people wouldn't miss
the train? He looked out of the door. There
was no sign of them. Oh dear – should he go
and hurry them up?

Meddle got out some pennies to give to the
children when they came. One fell from his
hand and rolled under the seat. Oh dear!
Meddle got down to get it. It was right in the
far corner. Meddle had to get half-way under
the seat to reach it.

A loud whistle blew. PHEEEEEEEE!
Meddle jumped. He tried to wriggle out from
under the seat, but somehow or other he got
stuck. 'Wait, wait! Tell the train not to go yet!'
shouted Meddle, from under the seat. But
nobody heard him, of course. The guard

blew his whistle again and then, with a rattle and a rumble and clatter, the train began to pull out of the station!

Meddle wriggled himself free and rushed to the window. He leaned out, shouting loudly, trying to open the door. It was a good thing he couldn't because the train was now going quite fast.

'Stop! Stop! Let me out!' yelled Meddle. 'I'm not going, I tell you!'

But he was. He couldn't help it! And the last thing that poor Meddle saw was the little man and his family all getting calmly into another train marked 'To Golden Sands' – and finding plenty of seats, too!

'This *wasn't* their train!' groaned poor Meddle. 'And *what* will the ticket inspector say to me if he comes and finds me without a proper ticket and all the seats to myself? Oh dear – this is what comes of helping people.'

No, Meddle – that's what comes of meddling! There he goes, all the way to the sea, first stop Seaside Town!